David Cuthbertson

Rosslyn Lyrics

David Cuthbertson

Rosslyn Lyrics

ISBN/EAN: 9783744796811

Printed in Europe, USA, Canada, Australia, Japan

Cover: Foto ©Andreas Hilbeck / pixelio.de

More available books at **www.hansebooks.com**

BY

DAVID CUTHBERTSON,

ASSISTANT LIBRARIAN, PHILOSOPHICAL INSTITUTION, EDINBURGH;

AUTHOR OF "ESKSIDE LYRICS."

Better for man
Were he and Nature more familiar friends.

ALEXANDER SMITH.

EDINBURGH:

THE EDINBURGH PUBLISHING COMPANY.

1878.

CONTENTS.

ROSSLYN LYRICS.

THE PIPER'S ADVENTURE.

A LEGEND OF ROSLIN.

Up above the sky was studded with the brilliant gems of
    night
Glitt'ring in a sea of azure, fair and wondrous to the sight ;
And the Pleiades shone faintly, while the Milky Way was
    seen,
With unnumbered lights attending, all robed in a pearly
    sheen.
Clear the moon shone, clad in brightness, sailing like a
    queen of air,
Shedding down to earth her splendour, beautiful beyond
    compare.
All around was wrapt in slumber, save the owl from out the
    glen,
Waking echoes with its crying thro' the woods of Hawthorn-
    den.
And the spirit of the breezes, wand'ring like a thing forlorn,
Roamed about, incessant crying for the day yet to be born.
Such a night as this there happened many hundred years
    ago,
When Will-o'-the-Wisp was dancing on the marshes to and
    fro.

A

In the dead of night, when demons walk the earth in ghostly
form,
When they gird a mantle round them, glide unnoticed
thro' the storm,
Came a Piper, playing boldly, thro' the woods of Hawthorn-
den,
Waking birds from peaceful slumbers, rousing echoes in the
glen.
And it seemed as if the spirits of the English dead, who fell
On the fated field of Hewin', near to old St Mungo's Well,
Followed thro' the night air screaming, in a wild and eildrich
tone,
Hovered round the valiant Piper, who kept up his constant
drone.
Past the Lover's Leap he wended, and a wraith here crossed
his path,
Faded in the leafy distance, silent in its very wrath.
Down the path below the Chapel, where St Clairs in armour
lie,
Slowly passed the Piper, playing where the Esk ran rippling
nigh.
Thro' the wicket, o'er the drawbridge, gallantly he held his
way,
While the stars looked down in wonder, and the moon gave
helpful ray.
Thro' a cavern, narrow, rugged, paced he playing valiant
still,
And the music sounded weirdly underneath the rocky hill.
At the vaults he ceased his playing, and there reigned a
silence grim,
While a thin veil covered all things with a misty vapour dim;
Clammy felt the walls around him, cobwebs all deserted hung,
While outside the breezes murmured, and their midnight
anthems sung.

Wand'ring carefully and slowly through the large ancestral
vaults,
Suddenly he paused in groping—for a moment's time he
halts ;
Then he lights a candle swiftly, peers adown towards his
feet,
While like muffled drums resounding, so his heart doth
quicker beat.
Carefully he scraped around him dust which had for ages
lain—
Dust perhaps of men and women, who in treachery were
slain ;
And a stone, with ring of iron, found he close beside the
wall,
And he tugged and pulled it upwards, let it sullenly back
fall.
Down he crept some steps beneath it, while his limbs all
shook with fear ;
But success lay just before him, soon would be wealth and
good cheer.
Here the passage widened outwards, like a crescent moon
'twas shaped ;
While the water trickled downwards from the walls with
dampness draped.
Up two steps into a chamber, where was seen a table old ;
On it lay a sword and bugle, with a mouthpiece of pure
gold ;
And a paper, old and fragile, lay upon the table there,
Which the Piper lifted gently, read the writing on't with
care—
Underneath this chamber treasure you will find, whoe'er you
be ;
But to gain such you must ring out on this bugle clear
blasts three.

Then the sword from out its scabbard you must whirl once
    round about,
Then the flags will rise up gently—quickly do this and not
    doubt.
Tremblingly the Piper lifted, from the table old and rare—
Blew a blast upon the bugle, waking spirits in the air ;
And it thro' the caverns wended, with an echo loud and long,
As the Piper blew another blast aloud both clear and strong.
But his heart it failed, and clammy were his hands and body
    all,
While the candle, burning dimly, cast strange shadows on
    the wall.
And he grasped the sword to wave it ; but, lo ! what a sight
    appears !
Knights who here had slept in quietness, for at least a
    hundred years,
Woke, and stood up in their armour, and the place was filled
    with light,
While around fair ladies wandered, lovely, beauteous to the
    sight.
Tables spread with viands reeking, wines which sparkled
    pure and clear ;
But a voice of thunder echoed—made the Piper quake with
    fear—
" Woe to you, false, helpless craven !   Better you had ne'er
    been born,
Than have tried and failed in sounding thrice upon the bugle
    horn."
Like the calm before a tempest, so a lull fell like a weight
Pressed upon the air around him, and the Piper met his fate ;
For a rumbling noise came swiftly, and the knights and
    ladies all
Vanished like a troubled vision, pass'd beyond all human
    call !

And the Piper still is waiting (so the wondrous legends
    say),
To come forth from out the Castle, and once more see light
    of day.
And at night oft in the winter, when the clouds hide stars
    from sight,
When the winds around are sighing, and the pale moon hides
    her light,
You can hear some wondrous music, standing on the wooden
    bridge,
Where the rocks are jutting forwards in a narrow, rugged
    ridge.
'Tis the sound of pipes resounding in the hollow ground be-
    neath,
Where above the grass is waving, with a coating thick of
    heath ;
And still yet a cave is standing, 'neath the Castle's ram-
    parts strong,
Where the Piper entered playing, and has waited there so
    long.
And the " Piper's Hole" folk call it, while the river passing by
Gurgles to the wind which hovers round the spot with plain-
    tive sigh.

LOST AND FOUND.

Snow had fallen all day long
    On the street and on the square,
    Cold and piercing blew the air—
Shrieking out defiant song.

And the snow-flakes, pure and white,
   Chased each other in affright ;
While above was seen no sky,
   Dull clouds brooded o'er the town—
Dark as midnight lingered nigh.

Underneath a lighted lamp
   Stood a woman singing there ;
   On her face and tangled hair
Crystal drops were shining damp.
   And she sang an olden song
   To th' unheeding, passing throng ;
And the plaintive air fell sweet,
   Rippled through the wintry air,
While her pulses swiftly beat.

'Twas not many years ago
   When she with her brother played,
   By the laughing meadows strayed.
Since those times much grief and woe
   Had she known, while in her heart
   Chords, long silent, break and part,
Leave her lonely in the night,
   Singing but a simple tune,
All around is wrapped in white.

Suddenly a passer-by
   Stood entranced the song to hear ;
   Paused, then went the singer near :
Like a whisper—as a sigh
   Something trembled on his tongue—
   Then a glance his accents rung—
" Sister !"—" Brother !" thus each said,
   While he, thankful, clasp'd the hands
Of her whom he thought long dead !

After many weary years
    Was the lost one found again ;
    Reconciled and left the pain
All behind, with terrors, fears.
    Never more was seen a form
    Singing clear 'mid snow or storm ;
For the wand'rer found a home,
    Where, with ev'ry want supplied,
She would never need to roam.

THE BUGLE CALL OF SONG.

WHEN the morning sun is shining, rising o'er the eastern hills ;
When each glen and valley echoes to the murmur of the rills ;
When the dewdrops glisten brightly on each blade of grass
    and flow'r,—
Sweet it is to walk and ponder at this quiet, early hour.
When the birds around are singing, Nature shows her
    choicest gems,
When she is but just awaking to give many diadems.
Nature ! thou that givest gladness, spreadest garments o'er
    the earth,
Making woods beside us echo with the joyfulness of mirth !
Nature ! thou that comest gaily when the winter's snows are
    o'er,
Tripping lighter than a fairy, bringing from thy treasured
    store
Snowdrops, crocuses, and daisies, wondrous flowers bright
    and rare ;—
Thou that givest treasures freely, modest, sweet, and ever fair—

Who would not delight to ramble in the peaceful, early
    morn?
When the sun is seen uprising, when another day is born!
Sing! ye birds, a joyful carol, let the glens resound with
    joy;
Sing! and make our hearts feel happy, tasting not the
    world's alloy.
Sing a song both clear and plaintive, rising high and falling
    low,—
Like the murmurs of the zephyrs when the western wind doth
    blow.
Sing, O river! gurgling, pulsing, threading ever on thy way;
Sing and tell to weary mortals of a future happy day.
Sing! and fill our hearts with laughter, make them all as
    bright and clear
As the sun reflected in thee sparkling on thy surface here.
Sing! and tell in noble language labour is not to be
    scorned;—
Better clad in garments modest, than with false gems be
    adorned!
Better to be working lonely, from the world and from her
    sight,
If we know, deep in our bosom, we are acting in the right.
Sing each bird, and tree, and flower, whisper gently in our
    ears;
Calm the doubts which rise within us, chase away all inward
    fears.
Let us look and think on Nature, working all around us here,
Decking many places grandly, making all things yet more
    dear,—
Dear to us, tho' life is fleeting, like the vapours now which
    rise
From the hills and valleys yonder, mounting upwards to the
    skies.

Song, however low and feeble, cheers us like a joyous smile,
Makes us happy for a little, and our cares doth oft beguile.
Each one here, however humble, has his duties to perform ;
Each one too must work and suffer, thro' the darkness and
thro' storm.
Soon the storms of life will vanish, soon we'll hear the sullen
roar
Break into triumphal music, on another brighter shore ;
And the music here so pleasant will be grander in that
clime,
When we've passed the golden portals, and have bade farewell
to time !
Oh ! my brothers, who are toiling downcast on this earth of
ours,
Life has many shadows in it, many days of rains and show'rs.
But with hearts that are determined, let us do the best we
can ;
Let us strive to rise aye upwards, and be foremost in the
van.
Let us sing the claims of labour, though our tasks be humble
all ;
Still, like soldiers, aye be marching, let our footsteps steady
fall ;
And then with the trump of gladness, and the bugle call of
song,
We will march forever forwards, with our hearts attuned and
strong.

A COUNTRY IDYLL.

SWEETLY sings the lark above me
    On this sunny day,
And he still mounts higher, higher,
While his voice ne'er seems to tire—
    Singing free and gay.
And the song comes downwards ringing,
With it memories many bringing
    As I gaze above ;
While I hear in all the singing
    Nought but love.

Clouds are floating past like phantoms
    In a garb of white ;
While they seem to chase each other,
Playing, sporting close together,
    Bathed in warm sunlight !
Till, at last, some of them sever,
Speed away just like a feather
    Till they're lost to view—
Speed away and bid forever
    All adieu !

Lovely violets and daisies,
    Modest, sweet to view,
Gaze shy up, as if appealing
To those having Nature's feeling
    For the pure and true.
And the Chapel in its glory
Seems to tell of some past story
    Of a greatness gone,
While it stands in sculptured beauty,
    And alone !

Zephyrs 'mong the leaves are whisp'ring,
    Humming soft a rhyme ;
All the woods around are ringing
To the sweet and dulcet singing,
    Like a hymn sublime.
All things join in Nature's chorus,
Beauty hovers round us, o'er us,
    Far away and near,
Making bright the path before us
    As we journey here.

ELAINE.

I.

WITH deep emotion,
And fond devotion,
I often think of
    My bygone years ;
And my thoughts turn ever
On her who will never
Return to me more—
    What use of tears ?
While my heart seems sighing,
And no voice replying
To thoughts that are flying
    Throughout my brain ;
But when no one is near,
I often can hear
Her voice that doth speak
    In plaintive strain.

II.

My memory dwells
Where I heard the bells
From the old church tower
   Ring sweet and clear ;
And methought while they rung,
That they chanted and sung
Of her who lives in
   A brighter sphere ;
And then a replying
Came surging and sighing
So sad, and then dying
   Softly away.
And her voice I did hear—
'Twas sweet to mine ear—
As she said, " Come now !
   Why do ye stay ? "

III.

And often at night,
As the fire burns bright,
When I think of her
   Who sweetly spoke,
Then Elaine comes cheering,
All doubts and fears clearing,
Bringing sweet thoughts of
   Life and of hope.
And ever and onward,
And upward and forward,
Her voice says, " Heavenward
   Come unto me ! "

Yes ! when no one is near,
Her voice I oft hear :
Ah ! soon we will meet,
   Elaine I'll see !

THE EMIGRANT'S HAME.

I.

I'M far frae hame ! I'm far frae hame !
   Frae Scotlan' an' her hills ;
I hear nae mair the lintie sing,
   Nor see the sparklin' rills.
My heart fills fu' wi' mony thochts,
   I feel a numbing pain ;
For boyhood's days are a' awa',
   They'll never come again.

II.

I'm far frae hame ! I'm far frae hame !
   Oot here I'm snell an' cauld ;
My hair is white wi' age an' care,
   I'm gettin' frail an' auld.
It seems just like a dream to me,
   I scarcely think it true—
But I am tott'rin' doun the brac,
   I'll sune be lost to view.

III.

I'm far frae hame ! I'm far frae hame !
  Frae Scotia's rocky shore—
Oh ! for a waucht o' caller air,
  An' sunny days galore !
Oh ! for a sicht o' heathery braes —
  To be at hame ance mair,
To meet a' roun' the ingleside—
  My faither in his chair.

IV.

I'm far frae hame ! I'm far frae hame !
  An' ilk ane I lo'e dear;
I feel at times a wean again,
  An' oft let fa' a tear.
Ay ! ay ! it costs us mony pangs,
  The ups an' douns o' life ;
It seems oor hale existence here
  Was just a'e roun' o' strife.

V.

I'm far frae hame ! I'm far frae hame !
  An' just like some auld tool
That's thrown aside, its day is dune—·
  I've served my time at schule.
An' now the young folk blithely laugh,
  An' ding the auld aside ;
Alack a day ! it's sad to think
  Hoo swift oor young days glide.

VI.

I'm far frae hame ! I'm far frae hame !
   An' gettin' wearied sair ;
I'm listenin' for the sough which tells
   'Twill sune be ower wi' care.
Oh ! gin my heart was young again,
   The warm bluid in my veins !
The hoast an' croichle oot my throat,
   An' supple were my banes !

VII.

I'm far frae hame ! I'm far frae hame !
   My sun is in the west ;
The nicht is comin' near at haun'—
   I'll sune be at my rest.
An' tho' a wanderer I hae been,
   Noo crippled, tott'rin', lame,
I hope to dwell wi' frien's again
   Abune, whaur is my hame.

BABY'S DEAD.

A JEWEL bright and rare
   Set in a casket frail ;
A form too fragile, e'er
   To stand a stormy gale.
A wee face white and pale,
   A pair of sunny eyes,
Which radiance often shed—
   But time all swiftly flies—
         Baby's dead !

Hands chubby, tiny, white,
   Clasped at her mother's knee ;
Words flowing out at night
   To Him of Galilee.
What beauties would she see
   In that bright realm of gold,
Since from the earth she's fled
   To join a better fold—
         Baby's dead !

A little prattling tongue
   That babbled music sweet ;
While in and out there rung
   A scampering of feet.
A joyous form to greet
   A mother's weary heart—
Who sees an empty bed,
   And feels a bitter smart—
         Baby's dead !

In distant, happy years,
   Would dark clouds roll away,
And banish all her fears
   With coming light of day ?
Who knows but what they may,
   And in the newer birth
She'll join alive o'erhead
   One who was loved on earth—
         Baby dead !

SONG—MAGGIE IS NEAR.

I.

I WILL travel the world in glee,
And forever happy I'll be ;
    Tho' the storms may roar,
    And the rain down pour,
For this is the reason why—
    Because ever near,
    To comfort and cheer,
My own love, Maggie, is nigh.

II.

Let the sun shine ever so fair,
'Twill chase away sorrows and care ;
    And then joys will flow
    Wherever I go,
And all things bright will appear ;
    For there is a face
    Where love I can trace,
For Maggie dear will be near.

III.

I will build a house of my own,
While in't I'll not dwell alone ;
    And there I will sing
    As glad as a king,
While want will ne'er enter my door ;
    And then a gay life
    I'll spend with my wife,
And what could a man want more ?

B

IV.

I'll plant in my garden with care,
Abundant flowers, exquisite, rare ;
 And there, oft at night,
 I'll walk with delight,
With one whom none can compare ;
 For where will you see,
 Wherever you be,
A flower like Maggie so fair ?

V.

Oh ! sweet will our lives ever be,
In all things we'll ever agree ;
 We'll never say " No "—
 That's naughty, you know ;
We'll be a model to all.
 And then if you come
 Near our happy home,
I'm sure you're welcome to call !

   ———

HE'S OVERHEAD.

WITHIN a mansion, stately, great,
 Where wealth had strewn her pearls fair,
A man, who owned a vast estate
 Of lands around, both rich and rare—
Whose hair was white with age and care,
 Was lying on a couch in state.

A sob at times broke on the air,
From one who felt it loth to part
With him, whose summer here had fled—
A whisper came from out his heart—
"He's overhead !"

The stars were twinkling clear and bright,
The moon looked down with sober face,
And shed abroad a silvery light,
Till all the landscape you could trace.
It was a lovely, pretty place,
In hallowed, sweet and tender night,
While everything breathed forth a grace,
Which told that love still lingered here,
And had not from the earth yet fled—
A prayer stole upon mine ear—
"He's overhead !"

A gentle breeze from o'er the hills
Was wafted by an unseen hand ;
It kissed the laughing, gurgling rills,
And flow'rs which grew in meadow-land.
And like an hymn, sublime and grand,
Which all the air with music fills ;—
Of strains, as from a heavenly band,
I heard a song, angelic, rare,
And ev'ry note quite plainly said—
Oh ! love makes all things ever fair.
He's overhead !

The stars all faded one by one,
As rising from her night of sleep
Aurora woke up with the sun,
And crystals from each flow'r did creep,

As if the sunshine made them weep
　　To see another day begun.
Its rays shone on the ocean deep,
　　The seabirds screamed aloud in glee ;
On earth and ocean each one read
　　As on a scroll, this written free—
　　　　　　　　He's overhead !

Fair children played about the bay,
　　Their laughter rippled by the shore,
And fled among the rocks away
　　Where shells lay piled—a goodly store.
And mothers thought of days of yore,
　　When all the world was light and gay,
For wondrous realms were them before—
　　Their hearts once more were full of love
Altho' their dazzling hopes had fled—
　　They knew that one reigned up above—
　　　　　　　　He's overhead !

On many graves the green grass grew
　　In yonder churchyard by the hill ;
And friends are getting still more few,
　　And places empty hard to fill.
The little joyous silvery rill
　　Kept prattling to the birds which flew
Around the old deserted mill
　　Of bygone times and other days ;
But still in all things it did blend,
　　And uttered oft, as if in praise—
　　　　　　　　He's overhead !

Throughout all Nature, ev'ry day
　　There runs a purpose firm and true ;

From early youth, so bright and gay,
 With hopes that time dispels from view,
Till life itself bids us adieu.
 Our early joys fleet fast away,
With gladdest things we ever knew—
 'Tis thus in every age and clime ;
And still this truth must ever spread
 Throughout the world till end of time—
   He's overhead !

AWAY IN THE WEST.

Away in the west a golden light's lingering
 Like to the wings of an angel of light,
Shedding a radiance of delicate fingering,
 And forming a world refulgent and bright.

And peacefully sleeping the hills seem enraptured,
 Catching a glory which comes from afar ;
While down at their base too, the ocean has captured
 A ray like a pure and glorious star.

Down in the valleys the grey mists are hovering,
 Thin cloudy vapours which linger a while ;
Slowly progressing, still stealing and covering
 The garlands of earth, till morning will smile.

Everything's beaming with great love and tenderness,
 Fitfully only the winds sob and moan ;
And 'mong the bushes are seen webs of slenderness,
 Gossamer threads which have fairylike grown.

Up in the heavens there dwelleth a holiness
  Which has imparted a calm to the earth ;
Speaking of happiness, while we in lowliness
  Wander in gladness from boisterous mirth.

There is a happiness, mingled with tearfulness,
  Thinking of years which have fled far away ;
While in our hearts we ofttimes have a fearfulness,
  Longing yet dreading the coming of day.

Thicker the gloaming comes down while we wondering
  Think of the beauties now veiled from our sight ;
Hid till the shadows of darkness are sundering,
  Soon will Aurora break forth with delight !

THE DILEMMA.

Sittin' lanely ! sittin' lanely !
  No a body near ;
Sittin' darnin' at my stockin's,
  Scarce a soun' you'll hear.
It is dreadfu', ne'er a lassie
  Wha will wed wi' me ;
Think you I am like a bogle
  That they frae me flee ?

Sittin' sewin' ! sittin' sewin' !
  Tho' my heart is sair,
Jaggin', bleedin' twa three fingers—
  'Deed I've plenty care.

What's come ower the bonny lassies
　　That I kent langsyne?
Dressed oot trigfu', brawly buskit,
　　Lookin' superfine!

Sittin' thinkin'! sittin' thinkin'!
　　What's this worl' to me,
If I canna get a lassie
　　Wha's a mou' to pree?
Hech! I feel just like a hermit
　　In this great big toun;
Nane to ask me hoo I'm keepin'
　　When I'm sair cast doun!

Sittin' lauchin'! sittin' lauchin'!
　　At a face I see,
Wha, I think, would hae some pity,
　　Be a frien' to me.
But I daurna tell my feelin's,
　　For I seem again
Like a wean wha tries the walkin'—
　　Canna gang alane.

Sittin' plannin'! sittin' plannin'!
　　Hoo to get a wife;
Ane wha'll keep me braw an' cheery
　　As I gang thro' life.
Tell me, then, ye sonsie lassies,
　　What a man should dae,
When he canna ask *the* question,
　　Tho' a wife he'd hae?

THE SABBATH DAY.

I.

I LOVE the quiet Sabbath day,
    When the psalm
In liquid music floats
Afar in air,
    Bringing a pleasing calm,
As birds from out their throats
Sing ever sweet and gay.
The wind blows softly where it lists,
    The running brooklets babble on their way ;
Upon the hills are filmy mists,
    Which float in masses gray.
A sacred stillness lingers in the air,
The world is all so bright and fair.
    While pearly diamonds gleam
        And sparkle bright
Among the flowers near—
    Like molten silver seem
        Unspotted to the sight.

II.

The people walk adown the street,—
    Faces glad,
Which tells of peace and love,
Full joyous sweet.
    But some pure eyes are sad,

And like the clouds above
Which now are sailing fleet
With shadows dark, so there's a gloom
  On their faces.
    And some are old,
Who soon must pass again to bloom
  Transplanted to the fold.
  But yet they know
With whom they oft have been,
  And who has washed each stain,
But whom they've not yet seen.

III.

Inside the kirk true prayers arise
  From a throng,
Whose fathers, good and brave,
Left happy ties,
  And sang in solemn song,
And prayed to One to save,
And make His word arise,
And usher in the blessed day
  When they no more, like beasts, would have to hide,
To steal, as branded men, away,
  But all in Him abide.
Their canopy was but the sky above
Which o'er them often smiled in love.
  And life some freely gave,
    Who lie at rest,
Whose names are still unknown,
  But, from many a grave
Fruit everlasting's grown.

IV.

Oh ! calm and hallowed Sabbath day,
    Ever dear ;
'Tis sweet to gaze at night,
When shadows gray
    Steal round us aye more near.
And in the house how bright
When fathers kneel and pray,
With children at their mother's knee,
  Who listen patiently to all that's said ;
While hushed are sound of mirth or glee
  As they hear a chapter read.
These are, indeed, the homes where dwells content,
Where ev'ry day are blessings sent !
  Oh ! Sabbath hours how sweet
    Art thou to me !
When all is fair around,
  And earth is smiling sweet,
For love this day has crowned !

CHILDREN'S LAUGHTER.

I.

I DELIGHT to hear the laughter
  Of the children when at play ;
For it makes my heart feel merry,
  And more lightsome all the day.

Like the ripples of the sunshine
　On a dark and dreary spot,
So are smiles from youthful beauty
　On an old man who's forgot.

II.

Like the singing of the zephyrs
　Through the leafy woods in June ;
Like the carol of the linnet,
　Or a sweet and welcome tune.
So I feel with children near me,
　For they chase all care away ;
While they leave sweet thoughts behind them,
　Make a weary heart feel gay.

III.

Oh ! I love to hear the laughter
　Which comes hearty, pure, and free,
Bringing back the days of childhood
　With an almost boyish glee.
I can see the purple heather
　On the far off Scottish hills,
And can hear the dreamy murmur
　From the clear and sparkling rills.

IV.

And like some majestic river,
　With its mirrored waters clear ;
So I love the children's faces,
　With desires that there appear.

And their chubby hands so tender,
  When I clasp them in mine own,
Make the whole world teem with beauty,
  And I feel no more alone.

V.

There is much in children's laughter—
  There's a balm for ev'ry sore—
When we hear their tiny footsteps,
  Then we love them all the more.
Yes ! the children are as flowers
  Blooming ever round us here ;
And their voices as sweet music,
  Tender, sweet, and ever dear.

THE LIBRARIAN'S CARNIVAL.

(IN THE COUNTRY—MORNING.)

THE sky was blushing
As clouds came rushing
Above the hill-tops
  In early morn.
While the birds were singing
Sweet memories bringing ;
And the woods were ringing
  For day was born !

All the rills were laughing
And happiness quaffing,
And gurgled with daffing
    While sparkling bright !
The lambkins went straying
Near branches swaying ;
West winds whispering
    Naught but delight !

(In the City—Morning.)

A fog was hov'ring,
The city cov'ring
With a mantle grey—
    A slender screen.
And the smoke was swirling,
And in long wreaths curling,
Like aërial feathers
    On high were seen.
Large rain drops were falling,
While carters were bawling,
And shouting, and calling
    With hoarse-voiced cries.
Many bells were ringing,
And workmen bringing
To toil and labour,
    For time aye flies.

(In the Country—Evening.)

Lassies were singing
And flowers flinging
As they wended home
    With faces bright.

And the lads were rushing
Where the waters gushing,
And sun's rays sparkled
    With golden light !
The cattle were wending
Their way slow, while blending
With daylight, and lending
    A sombre hue,
The dark shadows lengthened,
Deepened, and strengthened
As daylight faded
    And bade adieu !

(IN THE CITY—EVENING.)

The clouds were weeping,
While lamps were keeping
A watch like fire-flies
    With dull red gleams.
Deserted-like, dreary,
The city seemed weary,
Sleeping uneasily
    With troublous dreams.
And often a crying,
A sobbing and sighing
Of evil, came flying
    Throughout the air.
At times came a moaning
And muffled groaning
From creatures who once
    Were pure and fair.

Hurrah ! hurrah ! for a holiday,
  For a waft of the pure fresh air ;
For a few short hours in the country,
  When the flowers are blooming fair.

Hurrah ! for the green and grassy banks,
  For the smell of the scented thyme ;
To lie in the woods and hear the birds
  Singing songs which seem all sublime !

Hurrah ! for the hills where heather grows,
  And the heath with its purple bell ;
With the rocky crags, whose rugged sides
  Are all known to the shepherds well.

Hurrah ! for the beauties there revealed,
  For the calm which prevails o'er all ;
With the larks which carol sweetest song,
  And afar comes the plover's call.

Hurrah ! for a song when toil is done,
  For a treat down in Queen Street Hall ;
Where the night flies past with merry tales,
  Then hurrah ! for the Carnival !

Hurrah ! for the Carnival to-night,
  And hurrah ! for the merry songs ;
Hurrah ! for the laughter and the cries
  Which to this meeting aye belongs.

  Merry faces ! sober faces !
    Faces grave and bright !
  Plenty laughter, wit, and humour,
    Joyous is the sight !

Ladies whisper, eyes do sparkle
    Clear as liquid stars ;
Happiness o'er all is beaming,
    Nothing on it jars.

Hear the shouting and the clapping
    Down in Queen Street Hall ;
But we can excuse the crying,
    'Tis the Carnival !
Like a ray of golden sunshine
    On a lonely spot ;
So this meeting is a brightness
    On Librarian's lot.

We will enter.   Now we're seated,
    Scan the faces well,
Young and old Librarians plenty,
    Ages none can tell.
There are lady sup'rintendents,
    Cheeks yet pale and white ;
But they'll get some colour shortly—
    Carnival to-night !

There's the chairman, merry party,
    Ruddy face, blue eyes,
Smiles o'er all his face are rippling
    As if in surprise.
Hush ! he speaks ; it is a story
    Full of comic fun ;
Now the Carnival is opened,
    And the ball's begun.

Recitation—THE HUMOROUS CLERGYMAN.

A clergyman upon a tour,
In search of health and good air pure,
    Had travelled here,
    And wandered there,
In places wondrous, strange and fair ;
    By lovely glens,
    Through moors and fens,
And hamlets rural, sleepy, calm ;
    By gurgling burns,
    By lanes and turns,
Where lovely sights brought healing balm,
    And made his mind
    More still refined,
Communing with sweet Nature bright,
    Until he stood
    In happy mood
In that quaint town of Dunse one night.

In every place there is, I ween,
A character aye to be seen,
    Who shines by far
    Like some clear star,
Which glistens in a golden sheen ;
    And sparkles bright,
    A brilliant sight,
To all who gaze afar on high.
    And there was one,
    Named William Dunn
A man when people came him nigh,
    Would them beguile
    By winning smile,

C

And jokes which made the whole room ring ;
    Or tell a tale
    To make them pale,
And quite a weirdness round them fling.

This clergyman, then, after tea,
Asked if a barber he could see.
    The waiter ran
    And brought a man
Whose eyes were full of fun and glee.
    The shaving done,
    Then William Dunn
Commenced his jokes and tales so rare,
    Which chased that night
    With laughter bright
All sorrows far, and cankered care ;
    And wines were quaffed,
    While each one laughed,
And all went merry for awhile ;
    And quick and fast
    An hour went past—
But human nature's full of guile.

This clergyman had wit and fun,
As well's the barber, William Dunn ;
    He loved a joke,
    Could talk and smoke,
And with the young folk races run.
    And he could preach
    As well as teach
In language which all understood.
    So now, to-night,
    He felt quite bright,
And asked the barber as he stood

To go away,
If he would stay
And earn a guinea in a trice?—
    " 'Twont take you long,
    You're hale and strong,
Such chances don't come often twice.

" If you will jump o'er this chair here
For half-an-hour, and cry out clear,—
    ' Well, here goes I,
    My wife good-bye,
And ev'ry friend whom I love dear,'
    You will obtain,
    And by it gain
This guinea, so you can begin."
    The barber smiled
    As glad's a child,
And there resolved the coin to win.
    So, smiling gay,
    He hied away,
And then commenced to jump the chair ;
    And cried aloud
    As if a crowd
Stood round to see that all was fair !

For full ten minutes all went well,
As merry as a marriage bell.
    And William still
    Leapt with a will,
And felt more glad than tongue can tell.
    And " Here goes I,
    My wife good-bye,
And ev'ry friend whom I love dear,"
    Was still his cry,
    As time did fly

And brought his guinea aye more near.
　　But all in vain
　　He leapt to gain
The guinea which near to him lay—
　　Joys fleet and die
　　Like clouds which fly
Upon a sunny April day !

The clergyman, eyes brimming o'er,
Here rung the bell, when to the door
　　The waiter came,
　　His smile the same,
But stood amazed at the uproar.
　　" Now, sir, it's clear,
　　You'll cost me dear
By bringing such a fool in here,
　　And "—" Here goes I,
　　My wife good-bye,
And ev'ry friend whom I love dear."
　　Then o'er the chair
　　Will leapt with care,
Unheeding what the waiter said,
　　Who looked quite dazed,
　　With eyebrows raised,
Until, at last, he turned and fled !

Into the room the landlord came,
Wrath in his eyes, his nose aflame,
　　And with a stride
　　He stood beside
The barber, leaping still the same,
　　But " Here goes I,
　　My wife good-bye,

And ev'ry friend whom I love dear,"
    Was all he got
    From Will, who fought
And kept his course as yet all clear.
    When rushing in
    'Mid shouts and din
With eyes all red with bitter tears,
    His wife came fast
    And quickly cast
Her arms around him full of fears.

" Oh ! Willie, why this dreadfu' steer ;
Ha'e a' your senses left you here ?
    Oh !"—" Here goes I,
    My wife good-bye,
And ev'ry friend whom I love dear."—
    " What's wrang ava,
    Oh ! come awa,
The bairnies noo are a' asleep
    But little Kate,
    Wha sits up late
To meet you."   Here his wife did weep,
    And sobbed aloud
    Amid a crowd
Of people, who stood all around,
    Who sympathise
    With groans and sighs,
But William firmly kept his ground.

" My heart will break, come hame wi' me,
It's long since I ha'e mask't your tea.
    What's wrang ata' ?
    Oh ! come awa,

And stop your pranks--I'm like to die."
    But sweeping by
    He still did cry
The words so plain that all could hear—
    " Well, here goes I,
    My wife good-bye,
And ev'ry friend whom I love dear."—
    With brow of care,
    Will leapt the chair,
Determined now to do or die !
    His heart beat fast,
    As he oft cast
A glance to see how time did fly.

His wife her arms around him flung,
And to him earnestly she clung,
    And barred his way
    And made him stay,
While plying all her strength of tongue.
    Tho' William tried
    To push aside
Her arms, his course he had to stay ;
    And with a face
    Where you could trace
Vexation in a great degree,
    He turned about,
    And with a shout
Soon spoke aloud words bold and free.

" Oh ! wife, you've fairly done me noo,
But you've as muckle's me to rue !
    But let's gae wa',
    You're just a staw,

I've lost a gowden guinea new."
  And with a heart
  Just like to part
With sorrow, William hied away.
  But late that night
  All was made right ;
And he himself felt once more gay.
  And then away
  In early day
The clergyman of wit and fun,
  Was speeding fast,
  But often cast
A backward thought on William Dunn !

  As waves of the ocean,
  For ever in motion ;
  Now forwards, then backwards,
   Which never stand still.
  So surging and crying,
  The people defying
  Restraint of all kinds
   Broke forth with a will.
  No sleeping or napping,
  But cheering and clapping
  Of hands, with a rapping
   Of sticks, went on.
  And faces were beaming,
  With eyes brightly gleaming ;
  Joy reigned triumphant,
   All sorrows gone !
  But the chairman waving
  His hand, began craving
  Indulgence a little,
   As silence fell.

And like zephyrs sighing
Through the woods, came flying
A murmur dissenting,
    But all went well.
For a pretty creature,
Both in dress and feature,
And a silent preacher
    Of ev'ry grace,
Came forward 'mid cheering
Of people ne'er fearing,
And carolled sweetly
    With rosy face.

Song—THE DAYS THAT ARE GONE.

Air—"The Flowers o' the Forest."

I.

The day may be dreary, an' winds soughin' weary
And moanin', complainin' in Dryden's deep vales.
    And rains may be fallin',
    Wi' loud thunders callin',
And ilk thing aroun' me be trembling wi' gales ;
Sweet Nature a' sighing, clouds may be flying,
And spreadin' the heav'ns wi' their dark broodin' sails.
    Yet still I will treasure
    And think of wi' pleasure,
My Willie who cheer'd me wi' heart stirrin' tales.

II.

When the birds are singing, and the woods are ringing,
The sun o'er the Pentlands retiring from sight ;

And shadows are creepin',
In dark corners sleepin',
And fleecy clouds soarin' a' crimson and bright,
A glint o' my dearie kept me aye cheery,
And made my heart thud wi' a strange, fond delight.
Sae kind and forbearin',
Yet lovin' an' darin',
He stole a' my senses, and dazzled me quite.

III.

When gloaming descendin' comes down, and is blendin'
The beauties o' night wi' the garlands o' day,
I feel o'er me stealin'
A wonderful feelin',
And long to be rovin' wi' one far away.
But now, and for ever, my joys must sever,
Tho' yet I can hear him laugh happy and gay.
But pleasures are flying,
Then what use of sighing?
We grasp at a phantom, and can't make it stay.

She finish'd her singing,
And the Hall was ringing
With hearty plaudits
From one and all.
And then a Mechanic,
With face Titianic,
Came forth at the chairman's
Request and call.
His voice was sonorous,
And seem'd like a chorus,
It came rushing o'er us—
An unseen wave.

'Twas nought but a story,
With no deeds of glory,
But a simple tale,
To all he gave.

A Funny Mistake.

There's funny mistakes made ilk ane maun agree,
An' here is a story my faither tauld me
When I was a callan', an' ran 'bout the braes,
An' gather'd the brambles, an' sometimes the slaes.

Says my faither to me, " Weel, Geordie, ye ken,
Awa at the head o' yon bonnie wee glen,
Whaur the burnie comes doun wi' a lauchin-like soun',
As if a bit sang to itsel' it did croon ;
There lived in yon dwellin' which staun's a' its lane,
A woman who puir folk would never disdain,
Say frank aye an' hearty, a cheery bit wife,
Wha ne'er was in hot water ance a' her life.

A hard workin' body, she kept a braw coo,
A dog an' a cuddie, wi' hens no' a few ;
A pig which kept gruntin' throughout ilka day,
To chase for itsel' a' the silence away.

This wife was a widow, a couthy, braw dame,
Wi' twa bonnie callan's, but ane o' them lame ;
The ane drove the cuddie to market each day,
An' that—let me see, now—was three miles away.
An' aye the bit body she warstled awa,
An' kept her ain dwellin' aye dacent an' braw.

The minister ae day stept into her house,
They crackit awa baith fu' hearty an' crouse ;
They spak' o' the weather, the airt o' the win',
An' Adam's transgression, what led him to sin;
They spak' o' their neebours, o' Johnnie an' Kate,
Wha oft thro' the country stravaigèd gey late.
The widow she tauld him the price o' the meal,
An' spak' aye o' *somebody* wha wasna weel.
She mentioned her Tommy, an' spak o' her Will,
An' then (when near breathless), her scandal a' still,
She said her puir Robin was terribly bad
(She sighed unco deeply, looked up at him sad).
" No able for workin', he trauchles aboot,
An' roun' his sair leg I ha'e tied a bit cloot,
Wi' honey an' bees wax to mak' it hale sune—
But Robin, I'm doubtin', 'ill never mair run."

The minister wondered wha Robin could be,
For ane o' that name he ne'er minded to see.
Howe'er, ere depairtin', he sent up a prayer,
An' houped that this mishap would Robin prepare
To see that the pleasures o' life couldna last,
For time was aye comin' to ilka ane fast.
He prayed that a blessin' his sair leg micht prove,
An' oh ! may it please Thee, his illness remove.
He prayed for the widow, the Kirk, an' the State,
The rich an' the lowly, the puir an' the great.
He ended at last wi' a sort o' a sigh,
Then turned to the widow an' bade her good-bye.
The minister daun'ered awa' to his hame,
An' quickly in sicht o' his dwellin' he came ;
He entered it blithely, an' sat himsel' doun',
Removed frae his feet next his puir o' guid shoon,

Then on wi' his slippers, the tea was brocht ben,
Syne he spiert at the wife, " Noo, Mary, my hen,
Wha is't that's ca'ed Robin, wha lives i' the glen
Wi' Widow Macfarlane, for I dinna ken."

The wife cried out, " Robin ! losh ! wha can he be ?
But *Robin*, that's funny—but just stop a wee.
What for are ye spierin'? "   " Because he's no' weel—
I'm sure for oor neebours we aye ocht to feel.
I offered a prayer, when comin' awa,
Concernin' his illness—wha's Robin at a'? "
" I ken wha he's noo na.   You sent up a prayer !
I'm sure, weel, the next time, you'll need to tak care,
For just let me tell you—you're hardly to blame,
But Robin's *the cuddie*—you ocht to think shame."

Like two rivers meeting
And giving a greeting,
To flow on together
   United strong.
So there was a roaring
Of latent strength pouring,
From hundreds of voices,
   From out the throng.
It rippled, and flying
Unnoticed, went crying
Resistless and sighing
   With mighty strength.
But a silence falling,
At the chairman's calling
The Mechanic arose
   And spoke at length.

HEARING THE SERMON.

I'm sure you've heard tell o' wee bowed Jamie Spiers,
Who's been a Librarian for seventeen years ;
But yet he's a want o' respect for the Kirk,
As dour, on some points, as a hard driven stirk.

The minister cam' whiles an' crackit awa,
'Bout this thing an' that thing—'twould ne'er do at a' ;—
Tho' Jamie could argue, quote scraps o' queer Greek,
On points o' religion he seldom would speak.

However, it happened, he said he would gang
To the kirk if they'd sing a sensible sang,
Or gi'e him a sermon, an' ane that would keep—
Which needs must be lively, or likely he'd sleep.

When Sunday cam' round then, awa' Jamie went,
Ahint him the hale air was filled fu' o' scent ;
While mony folk giggled an' stared in surprise,
An' turned up the whites o' their een to the skies.

I dinna ken hoo it was, Jamie was late,
But some would ascribe this, like Moslems, to Fate,
An' gang awa sighin' an' shakin' their heads—
I think there's in this worl' just ower mony creeds.

Neist mornin' I met him gaun rowin' alang,
His legs, like his voice, had been years off the fang.
I spoke to him blithely, an' asked for his hens,
His sheep an' his grunters, an' gudeness a' kens.

The Kirk it came next. When I asked him the text,
The body looked puzzled, an' seemed to be vext ;
But sune he made answer, an' said, " I was late ;
What could a text matter ?—I liket my seat."

Thinks I to mysel', noo this looks unco queer,
But I shall no' stop tho', but something else spier ;
So "what did he wind up wi', Jamie?" quo' I—
At this he emitted a dolorous sigh.

" I'll tell you the truth, I was late o' gaun in,
An' heardna the minister his wark begin ;
So tiring o' listenin', I slippit awa
Afore he was done,—couldna stand it at a'."

" Please tell me then, Jamie, what was't that he said
The time you were in ?"—Here he hung down his head.
" As sure as I'm leevin', 'twas doubtless sublime,
I ne'er heard a word o't—*I slept a' the time !*"

Attitudinising
Went on, ev'n surprising
The Mechanic himself,
   Who often smiled.
But Jamie was glooming,
'Mid fair faces blooming,
And blushing with roses,
   For he felt "riled."
His glances went stealing
With rancorous feeling ;
While his brain seemed reeling
   With ire suppress'd.
But an old man beaming
With smiles, and seeming
A happy being
   Now us address'd.

Recitation—OOR STAIR.

It's a wonderfu' place, I ween,
 The fit o' oor entry at nicht,
When there's scarcely a mune to be seen,
 An' hardly the glint o' a licht.
You're aye sure to find a bit lass
 Wi' a face to match a red rose—
Altho' it be frosty and cauld,
 Hard enough to freeze ony nose.

It's something like near thirty years
 Since first I got married, ye ken ;
Hech me ! it oft seems like a dream,
 To think o' the time gane since then.
To tell you a secret or twa—
 But dinna gi'e me such a stare—
My Sarah and I met each nicht,
 Doon by at the fit o' the stair.

We had nae long walkings at nicht,
 Stravaigin' awa here an' there ;
Tho' sometimes we'd tak a bit jaunt
 By green fields and breath the fresh air.
At last we got married, an' noo
 I've weans, but what do they care ?
They're grown up, an' meet (like oursel's
 Langsyne) at the fit o' the stair.

An' sometimes I hear a bit smack,
 An' syne a bit geegle or twa ;
Hech ! I wish my young days were back,
 But time's stown them noo a' awa'.

Yet still I am happy—content,
　　Ye ken, we should never despair ;
There's *ane* wha's bit mou' I whiles pree,
　　As I did langsyne at the stair !

An' lasses and lads will aye meet,
　　An' love will aye ha'e its ain way
Till they get a house o' their ain,
　　An' *that* tak's gude money to pay.
Still I like to see the bit lads,
　　Their lasses decked out braw an' fair,
Whispering joyous, while standin'
　　For hours at the fit o' the stair.

　　But sin is defiling,
　　So Jamie was smiling
　　As he stept up quickly
　　　　On to the stage.
　　And around him glancing
　　He saw bright eyes dancing
　　With fun, which filled him
　　　　With inward rage.
　　Like an old branch swinging,
　　And ghostly fears bringing,
　　Or as cracked bell ringing
　　　　So seem'd his voice ;
　　And we listen'd amazed
　　(A few of us dazed)
　　While he spoke aloud—
　　　　His theme, new choice.

THE MECHANICAL MAN.

A youngish chiel wha ance was braw,
A man whom Nature made a staw—
                    Librarian X.

His footsteps fa' wi' thumpin' clash,
As if the floor he fain would smash—
                    Librarian X.

His face is long, his een are sma',
An' scarce a wink he sees at a'—
                    Librarian X.

He peers into ilk body's face—
His ain is aften oot its place—
                    Librarian X.

He gangs wi' hands ahint his back,
An' keeps us ever on the rack—
                    Librarian X.

An' whiles he tries to hum a sang,
His voice, alas ! is aff the fang—
                    Librarian X.

He sometimes tries to whistle too,
But he has little else to do—
                    Librarian X.

He whummles here and wanders there,
As if ower a' he took gude care—
                    Librarian X.

D

He shuns the books, but counts his "tin"—
We ca' him aft a man o' sin—
                    Librarian X.

We dae the wark, he tak's his rest,
For, oh ! he lo'es the money best—
                    Librarian X.

He flytes as gude's an auld fishwife,
But he himsel' keeps oot o' strife—
                    Librarian X.

An' at his nose whiles hangs a drap,
A fozey, thowless-looking chap—
                    Librarian X.

There's mony men we a' could want,
An' there is ane whom nane could daunt—
                    Librarian X.

We wish he'd tak his wizzened face
Frae oot the toon an' leave the place—
                    Librarian X.

But ills we here maun suffer a'—
There's ane we canna thole at a'—
                    Librarian X.

Still we will trust to see him gang
Frae us awa'—he's lived ower lang—
                    Librarian X.

Like the thunder crashing,
So past us came flashing
A book with a whizzing,
　　Which dashed swift by.
It struck Jamie standing,
And on his face landing,
It made his eyes sparkle
　　Like stars on high.

Others came hurrying
While leaves were flurrying,
Everywhere scurrying,
　　Over the hall.
And Jamie replying,
Returned books shying
With aim unerring—
　　Bright Carnival !

Librarian X stood
In his injured manhood,
And book after book went
　　Straight to the mark.
Jamie's eyes were swelling,
And salt tears were welling,
While people were leaving—
　　The hall now dark.

Like a great wind sighing,
And sobbing, and crying,
Still missiles went flying
　　Till all were done.
And then each retreated,
Neither defeated,
Confident both had
　　The victory won.

As each one home wended
From Carnival ended,
They talked to each other
   In merry strain.
As the stars were shining,
The moon seemed reclining
On cloudlets phantomlike,
   Pure, without stain.

The Tron bell was ringing,
And zephyrs were singing ;
While the lamps were flinging
   A lustrous light.
Farewell ! to the meeting,
Time's flying—is fleeting ;
And shaking your hands,
   We say Good-night !

LASSWADE REVISITED.

RAMBLING once more in the village olden,
  Where many a happy day was spent ;
Where now, from on high, the sun's rays golden
  Shine on the spots I loved to frequent.
I think of the time when school was over,
  As I ran with comrades glad at play ;
And tho' I have wandered, been a rover,
  Rarely have I been so blest and gay.

There is the river, flowing on ever,
   Its waters tinged with a murky red ;
Where the moonbeams love at night to quiver,
   As the clouds sail stately overhead.
Playmates many, the good and true-hearted,
   Have pass'd with a song to joys unseen ;
While I am here, who with them have parted,
   Of my boyhood friends alone I glean !

Passing the school I can hear fresh voices
   Singing a song to an old quaint tune ;
And my heart within me yet rejoices,
   For sadly I feel tho' life's at noon.
My youthful years have been as the sighing
   Of winds which have sped and died away ;
And left me now with an inward crying,
   While the salt tears dim mine eyes to-day.

Down in my breast there's a strange emotion ;
   I seem to stand in my class once more,
And hear a noise like that of the ocean
   When dashing against a rock-bound shore.
O dear old days ! how for them I'm longing—
   Days which are gone, yet I wish again ;
And still fond memory's fount is thronging
   With bygone thoughts, tho' of joy and pain.

Silence lingers, and is now unbroken,
   The village seems to sleep and dream ;
Telling to none, and giving no token
   What is the pleasing or mournful theme.
The world moves round, and dear ties must sever,
   Our hearts get refined with grief and pain ;
We would keep the sweets and leave them never,
   Yet a gladness cometh after rain.

And still, Lasswade ! I in fancy linger
　　When far away, in thy village calm ;
And I often hear a sweet harbinger—
　　The solemn chant of an evening psalm.
The shadows creep, and the night is blending,
　　And clasping hands with departing day ;
While stars peep forth, all their beauty lending,
　　As I slowly wend from thee away.

MY SISTER AND I.

I'M no' often angry, an' rarely you'll meet
A lass like mysel' wi' a temper as sweet.
I'm wee, but folk tell me the best o' a' gear
In sma's is weel boukit, so nane need me jeer.

My face is gey bonnie, weel-featured, ye ken,
It pleases mysel', an' it smiles on the men.
My sister torments me, an' drives me near mad,
Because I whiles speak to a dacent bit lad.

Noo, just to speak plainly, ha'e sense for a wee,
What's wrang wi' my sister aft whiles puzzles me
She's aulder than me tho', an' bonnie an' a',
An' yet she's still single—the men are a staw !

Some lads they will gang wi' a lass wha's a face
Like a washed-oot bit cloot, ne'er think it disgrace.
The heart is a problem, plays won'erfu' pranks,
An' Cupid, the rascal ! gets very few thanks.

I dinna like talkin' awa 'bout mysel'
(My sister whiles tells me my tongue's like a bell)—
She's gifted hersel, na, can talk braw an' crouse,
When I'm sittin' silent, as quiet as a mouse.

There's a callan' I ken—a braw, comely chiel—
Weel featured an' dacent, gude-lookin' atweel ;
I think he's a fancy to me na himsel'—
But man is as fickle as woman hersel'.

I whiles get a paper, a book at odd times,
An' in them are written the funniest rhymes ;
They set me oft lauchin', my sister an' a',—
I'm like to split aften, maist roun' as a ba'.

I think I've a weakness for ane like himsel,
He keeps aye sae cheery, just like my ainsel.
My sister aye bothers an' pesters me sair,
An if 'twasna for him, I'd dee in despair.

Love's stronger than water, an' thicker than bluid.
An' folk while in this state, forget to tak fuid ;
My sister's no married, I think I can see
What mak's her sae angry tormentin' aye me.

Because she's no married, she wants to keep me
Awa frae my sweetheart, but that will ne'er be ;
Whenever he asks me to keep his bit hoose,
I'll craw ower my sister, baith hearty an' crouse.

THE PENTLAND HILLS.

I CAN hear the flute-voiced plover
  'Mong the purple heath-clad hills,
    Crying clear,
    Sweet to hear,
  Just beside the laughing rills,
    As they foam,
    And do roam
  Through the glens all lovely, calm,
  Where in days gone by one saw
  Sights which filled stout hearts with awe ;
    Yet arose
    'Midst great woes,
  The solemn chant of martyr's psalm !

Heathery hills, steeped in grandeur,
  Could you speak what tales you'd tell !
    Great deeds done,
    Vict'ries won,
  With the cries of those who fell—
    Men who wrought,
    Nobly fought,
  To put down a tyrant's cause.
  And their blood was freely shed,
  Thousands mingled with the dead—
    Gained the crown
    Of renown.
  Ere dawned upon them freedom's laws.

Rullion Green, once famed in story,
  Underneath thy sod there lies

Martyrs brave—
Men who gave
Hearts as well as kindred ties !
But tho' dead
There has sped
From their lives a forward wave
Of religion, which yet sweeps
O'er the land that treasures, keeps
Thoughts of those
In repose,
Sleeping quiet in unknown grave.

Joy and sorrow meet together
As I wander here and there.
While I seem
In a dream—
Everything's so bright and fair.
Peace now reigns,
Happy swains
Wander in their youthful love ;
All is calm,
Bringing balm
With peace around and up above !

THE RAIN.

(After E. A. Poe's "The Bells.")

SEE the falling of the rain—
April rain !
Coming gently downwards to refresh the earth again.
And you hear it pittar-patter
'Mong the leaves which clothe the trees.

While the sparrows chirp in chorus,
As the shower keeps pouring o'er us,
  In delight, as if to please.
  " I have more, more, more
  For you people yet in store "—
Seems to say a million voices in a delicate refrain
  From the rain, rain, rain, rain,
   Rain, rain, rain,
Falling everywhere in forest, glen, and plain !

See the mist which cometh down
   From the hills !
Rolling swiftly o'er the country, kissing all the rills.
  Onward, onward, thus it goes,
  While the west wind softly blows.
  Then hear the crows
  Holding converse 'mong the trees,
In a language neither pleasant nor in tune,
   Goodness knows !
  While the mist it soaks us through
With its nasty, penetrating, thorough drenching dew—
  Mountain dew
   Ever new,
  Caring not for girl or boy,
  But in all it seems to joy,
  And delights to make us hasten
  (They can stay who list).
Oh ! the mist, mist, mist, mist,
What discomfort oft it gives us, doth the mist !

See the heavy drops of rain,
   Thund'rous rain !
And the clouds are speeding quickly 'bove the plain.
  Soon you hear the thunder roar,
  Louder than the waves at shore,

In a deaf'ning stunning peal,
  Which makes some frighten'd feel,
   At the sound.
All the heavens darken'd o'er us, covered up with solemn pall,
As th' artillery goes crashing, making heavy rain drops fall.
   How they glisten, glisten, glisten,
   While people listen, listen
  To the peals which come in crashes
  Close behind lightning flashes—
Fire and air in great commotion !
  While the rain, rain, rain,
  Seems the thunder to disdain,
   For it pours.
  And along the gutters wide
  Flows a dark and turbid tide ;
And it eddies back and forwards at its shores.
  Till at last its wrath is spent,
   And in sorrow
   Seems to borrow
  Penitent a little light.
And the sun peeps thro' the clouds,
  As the thunder hies away,
   With a rumble
   And a grumble
  Like an enemy at bay.
And the air is cool and pleasant, while the birds sing sweet
  again
   To the rain.
  Thund'rous rain, rain, rain, rain,
   Rain, rain, rain—
All the earth rejoices, smiling o'er the rain.

THE AULD FOLK.

I.

THE kind auld folk I kent langsyne
    Are deein' fast awa ;
An' slidin' gently doon the brae,
    Wi' hair as white as snaw.
I liked to hear them crack awa,
    Fu' couthie, frank, an' free ;
An' tell about their former days,
    Wi' half a boyish glee.

II.

Ay ! ay ! the auld folk quickly gang,
    An' fade frae oot oor sicht ;
Their gude auld-farrant tongues nae mair
    We hear them wag at nicht ;
An' bonnie weans, wi' curly hair,
    Wha lo'ed their granpa weel ;
Each learn the frost o' early spring—
    First sorrows when they feel.

III.

The dear auld folk wha sat beside
    The ingleside at e'en ;
Hoo mony lie beneath the sod ;
    Hoo mony graves are green !
Oor hearts a stounin' pain aft feels,
    To think nae mair we'll hear ;
The honest, hearty phrase of truth,
    An' kindly word o' cheer.

IV.

We wander but-an'-ben the house,
  Fu' dowie, doun wi' care—
For oh ! we miss the dear auld folk,
  We see the empty chair.
Ay ! there's the Book they lo'ed sae weel,
  An' aften used to read ;
An' there's the stick,—a trusty frien',
  Which never mair they'll need.

V.

We gang beside each glen an' brae,
  We kent in days gane by ;
An' wander up an' doun the street—
  Ah me ! how time doth fly !
Familiar forms how few we meet
  Beside the ripplin' burn—
It's strange hoo mony folk we miss,
  Which ever way we turn.

VI.

The auld kirkyaird is quiet an' still,
  Where dead in silence lie ;
The wind moans by the grassy graves,
  With plaintive, moaning sigh.
The bairns aft pluck the gowans sweet,
  Frae aft their juicy stem ;
The auld folk are a' wede awa
  To grace His diadem.

VII.

A blessin' on the leal auld folk,
　Whose cares are ower at last ;
They've warstled oot the road awa',
　A peace they've gained at last.
Then kindly speak where'er you be—
　To auld folk aye be true ;
For age is takin' them awa',
　An' comin' fast to you.

———

THE SPIRIT OF NIGHT.

Sin woke from her slumbers deep,
From a dreamless, golden sleep ;
　　And her eyes were bright,
　　Of a ruby light—
She never could sigh nor weep.
　　And her face was fair,
　　And made to ensnare
The people o'er all the earth.
　　She was always young,
　　And her accents rung,
In the very haunts of mirth !

The stars were studding the sky,
And glittering pure on high ;
　　As there sped a ray
　　Like the light of day,

As the form of Sin went by
   In a robe of white
   With emeralds bright,
But the wind with plaintive sigh,
   And a long-drawn moan,
   In sorrowful tone,
Wept aloud with anguish sore,
   For it knew that Sin
   Where she entered in,
Left misery evermore !

On her forehead gleam'd a light—
A diamond which glitter'd bright,
   And shone like a star,
   'Twas seen from afar ;
For Sin loved beautiful night.
   For it hid her deeds,
   All her vile misdeeds ;
And covered them up from sight.
   Yet her cruel face
   Has a wondrous grace,
To lead men from truth and right.

She left a terrible stain,
Followed by anguish and pain
   Wherever she went.
   All her time was spent
In adding men to her train.
   The rich and the poor
   She both made impure,
And smiled while she wrought the ill ;
   And her heart, alas !
   Was as hard as brass,
And no tears could change her will.

Into a cottage she crept
Where a creature worn-out slept,
 And adown his cheeks
 There were seen dark streaks,
For long and bitter he'd wept
 O'er his awful sin,
 Tho' he strove to win,
And steal from the fiend away;
 But she held him tight
 Far away from sight,
And he own'd no other sway.

He woke with a start to feel
His hands were as cold as steel,
 And his brow was wet
 With a cold damp sweat—
For him was it woe or weal?
 Sin stood for awhile
 With a fitful smile,
Then laughed o'er what he had lost!—
 Oh! that men would turn
 And the demon spurn,
And think of the awful cost!

And he cried aloud in vain,
In his misery and pain;
 And visions arose
 To check his repose,
While a fire burned in his brain.
 "Oh! where shall I find
 A balm for my mind—
Is there such a thing as rest?
 Is there none to hear,
 Not any to cheer,
The man who hath friends is blest!"

And Sin stole silent away
To haunts degraded yet gay ;
 And into each heart
 She sent a keen dart,
And smiled in demonlike way ;
 For the world she knew,
 And her subjects too,
Who strove in their might to break
 From her bondage dear,
 With its dread and fear,
But she would not them forsake.

Into a carpeted room,
Sin came in the midnight gloom,
 And she saw a form
 That had stood life's storm,
Now sinking towards the tomb ;
 And he heard the roar
 From the other shore,
For the rising tide was near.
 And his hair was white,
 He had fought the fight,
And vict'ry soon would him cheer.

Sin whisper'd words in his ear,
And tried to fill him with fear ;
 But he strove to pray,
 To chase far away
The thoughts that were surging clear ;
 And he struggled long,
 For his faith was strong,
But the wicked words came fast ;
 And a weary sigh
 Came swiftly by,
Borne hurriedly on the blast.

E

He strove in the awful fight
('Tis hard to keep in the right)—
    And the sweat amain
    Fell down as the rain,
Yet still he steered for the Light !
    Tho' wretched and worn,
    With doubtings, fears, torn,
He cried for help from above—
    'Tis hard to be near
    The beauteous sphere
And hear no accents of love !

But Sin arose in affright,
And shrank at a solemn sight ;
    For into the room
    There came in the gloom,
Faith, Hope, the twin sisters bright.
    And they *looked* at Sin
    As they entered in,
With horror both in their eyes ;
    And Sin fled amazed
    Like a being dazed—
As stars peeped down from the skies.

Oh ! Sin is a deadly thing,
And leaves behind it a sting
    That forever grows
    Into greater woes
Wherever her false notes ring.
    She wanders and flies,
    But heeds not the cries
That go from earth to heaven.
    There still is a balm
    Which bringeth a calm—
Those who repent are forgiven.

And Sin in the world still flies
In many a strange disguise ;
 And she whispers still
 Of evil and ill
Wherever her work she plies.
 And she hates the true,
 And longs to imbue
Each one with her deadly stain.
 Oh ! Sin is a foe
 Leaving naught but woe,
And misery, anguish, pain !

A NIGHT PICTURE.

I.

UPON the rippling tide we sped,
Our noble bark went swift and free,
 The moon shone clear,
 And shimmered near
In feathery flakelets on the sea.
 While stars above
 Revealed a love
With golden orbs, in depths of blue,
 Which seemed to smile,
 And all beguile
By what they there displayed to view.

II.

The clouds afar in vapours white,
In tiny masses soared on high,
    And spread in air
    Their beauties fair,
Like snowflakes close against the sky.
    And as a sigh
    Which comes us nigh,
The west wind blew with whisper soft
    And kissed the sea
    In very glee,
And moved the pennon up aloft.

III.

Reflected in the depths below
The fishes swam and glittered bright.
    All mirrored there,
    Surpassing fair,
Like lustrous globes of golden light !
    And, as they gleamed
    And sped, it seemed
As if one caught a glance where dwelt
    The mermaids all
    In coral hall,
For round us shone a quiv'ring belt.

IV.

And floating calm upon the tide,
The sea anemones were seen
    In colours grand,
    As if a hand
Had touched them with a fairy sheen.

Red, white and blue,
Of varied hue—
As pearls beauteous to the sight,
They gleamed below
With wondrous glow,
And added splendours to the night.

v.

The foam glanced from the vessel's side,
And rippled o'er the glassy sea.
From far away
A thin mist, gray,
Came stealing noiseless on our lee.
While breezes slept
It nearer crept,
And covered all with slender veil,
Which hid the light
Of tender night,
That passed away as joyous tale.

THE HAVEN IN THE FUTURE.

I WAS sitting thinking—dreaming of my boyish days of yore,
Happy times for ever vanished that will come to me no
more.
Deep within me hidden feelings stirred my heart and made
it glow,
When I thought of friends departed—of great sorrows and of
woe.

Backwards went my fancy fleeting, and I fought my battles
    o'er,
All elate with youth's ambition, as I pushed my barque from
    shore ;
And the world, what cared I for it !--thought that life was
    always bright,—
Little thinking, little dreaming, of the stern-contested fight !
But the time rolled on full quickly, each year seemed to
    swifter fly,
And I felt so faint and weary that I almost wished to die ;
For great trials pressed upon me, bore me down and made
    me weak,
That I sought a quieter haven, better refuge tried to seek.
Long I struggled, battled bravely, till grown old I lay me
    down,
Push aside all vain ambition, give up striving for renown,
And I try to pierce the future, tear the veil which hides my
    view,
Long to draw away the curtain that divides the false from
    true.
But I cannot ; so I'm waiting till I hear my Master call
From the haven in the future, where no sorrows ever fall.
So I'm working—doing something—for I soon shall pass
    away
To that place where all is gladness—to that land as bright as
    day.

HAWTHORNDEN.

SCENES of splendour and of grandeur,
Where the Esk loves to meander,
Sparkling here and speeding ever,
Gurgling, pulsing, stopping never ;
Through the glen it goes on stealing
Where are beauties worth revealing,—
Flowers many freely blooming
In their dress all unassuming.

See the sun's rays clearly shining
On the leaves with golden lining ;
While the butterflies keep flitting,
And the bees are honey sipping.
Birds around are ever singing,
Through the wood their notes are ringing ;
While the wind keeps gently sighing—
Telling all that Time is flying.

Hawthornden ! where Drummond wandered,
And on all thy beauties pondered ;
Where he wrote his gentle verses,
Which to all this day rehearses,
That he had a poet's vision,
Mingled with a rich fruition,
That comes yet adown the ages,
Bearing truth on all its pages !

" Rare Ben Jonson" here once sported,
And with Drummond muses courted.
Spirits sweet ! ye met and parted,
Gifted brothers, leal, true hearted !

Hawthornden, tall trees surround thee,
Stately beauties linger round thee ;
Where sweet Nature has expended
Many charms and finely blended.

Sing, ye winds, now gently sighing !
Sing, oh ! river, in replying ;
Sing, ye birds, a noble chorus,
That will cheer our path before us !
Oh ! long may thy beauties linger,
And may Time's all ruthless finger
Gently deal, and leave sweet traces
On thy best, most treasured places !

FORGET-ME-NOTS.

I.

FAIR FLORA came with garlands sweet,
And flow'rs sprang up beneath her feet.

The hills no more were white with snow,
While lambs went frisking to and fro.

The gurgling burn was pure and clear,
And threading on thro' glade and mere.

The sky above was blue, while clouds
Kept flitting past like infant shrouds.

Two sweet forget-me-nots one morn
I saw a little crest adorn.

I looked into their starry eyes—
An emblem they of paradise.

II.

Two little girls came hand in hand,
Like fairies from an unknown land.

Two pairs of hands, four hazel eyes.
Two faces full of glad surprise.

III.

I passed again along that way,
Where in the morning all was gay.

The mavis high on yonder tree
Was singing clearly, bold and free.

The clouds were tinged with rosy glow ;
The wind was sighing to and fro.

The sweet forget-me-nots which grew,
Had vanished like the morning dew.

But further on I saw them lie
Beneath night's calm and azure sky,

All withered, faded, torn, and dead—
Their brief short term of life had fled.

IV.

Two short months passed, and then I saw
A sight which filled me half with awe.

In yonder churchyard, near the wall,
Where all the day the sunbeams fall,

Two little graves (and underneath
The white and spotless, modest wreath),

Lay silent now, two babes at rest,
Who never more would feel unrest.

A SCOTTISH WIFE.

THE win' is soughin' doun the lum, outside I hear the rain
Come wi' a constant pit-a-pat against each window pane.
An' Donald's out upon the hills, a wild an' eerie place,
When clouds are scourin' up abune, the pale mune hides
    her face.
It's lanely sittin' here mysel', an' no a body near,
Wi' fancies flittin' thro' my brain, within me awsome fear.
My heart maist loups into my mou' whene'er I hear a cry,
For in each thud or soun' there is an eildrich lonesome sigh.
There's mony folk beside mysel' whose heart feels aften drear,
An' I would be the blithest lass, if Donald were but here.
I love my Donald's ringing laugh, wi' soun' as clear's a bell ;
An' oh ! I love his handsome face, but best o' a' himsel'.

An' when he grups my haun' in his, he gie's it such a squeeze,
It brings the tears oft to my een—I'm never ill to please.
But, whisht! was that the collie's bark I heard doun i' the
   glen?
I'll stir mysel' an' mask the tea,—the fire I'll need to men'.
For Donald lo'es a trig bit house, wi' a' things braw an' clean,
Wi' plenty bannocks i' the press, an' aitmeal cakes a wheen.
I'm sure the auld days were the best, when Scotland fed her
   men
On weel-baked scones an' guid aitmeal—but what a fa' since
   then !
You'll seldom see a parritch pat, or even peasemeal brose—
Ay ! that's the food which made our men, so famous, I
   suppose
For strength, an' heicht braw buirdly chiels wi' een aye clear
   as day,
An' hearts which were aye true as steel—are th' auld times a'
   away ?
Ah ! there's the outer yett blawn wide, a reeshle at the door,
There's Donald's haun' upon the sneck—outside a sullen roar
An' he himsel' steps blithely in, wi' collie at his side.
Ay ! love is best where it is seen just at the ingleside.

SITTING BY THE FIRE.

WHEN sitting by the fire,
   And thicker grows the gloaming,
My thoughts ne'er seem to tire,
   But always go a roaming.
      I see the land,
      Sublime and grand—

The hills with purple heather,
    And friends I knew
    Now grown so few
I sported with together.
   Yes ! when I sit alone,
I on the past oft ponder ;
   While I, grown old, unknown
Am left behind to wander.

Our youth can not remain,
   For years come onward stealing ;
They bring at times a pain,
   And sometimes happy feeling.
     And joys won't last,
     But fleet as fast
As clouds which float in ether.
     Oh ! life and truth,
     And joyous youth,
And happy summer weather !
A pain is at my heart
   When fancy, backwards hieing,
Recalls up with a start,
   How quick the time's been flying.

When sitting by the fire,
   I sometimes see a vision,
And hear as from a lyre,
   That hope has reached fruition.
     But 'tis a dream,
     A passing gleam
Of sunshine on my sadness.
     For winter's near,
     My life is sere,
Griefs mingle with my gladness.

Oh ! happy boyhood's years,
  And days which knew but pleasure,
I think of them with tears,
  And thoughts of them I treasure.

Yet, flitting ever near,
  Some spirits keep aye singing
A song I ever hear,
  Like wedding-bells a ringing.
      Sweet and sublime,
      In fairy rhyme,
It swells, and falls receding—
      Now soft and low,
      Then to and fro,
Aye fancy onwards leading.
The daybreak is at hand,
  The Day Star is appearing,
And shining o'er the land,
  To which our bark is steering.

THE SOLDIER'S REWARD.

WORN out, exhausted, and dying
  By the heat of battle and strife,
A wounded soldier lay silent,
  And bidding farewell to this life.
Around him the watch-fires burning,
  Cast a weird and solemn like glow ;
While he heard his heart go throbbing—
  Monotonous, faintly, and low.

Beside him the river murmured, while it throbbed and sang
　　on its way
A song triumphant and joyous, as his life was fleeting away !
His thoughts went back to the village, and he dreamt he sat
　　in the choir,
While the summer sun was sinking o'er the hills in a globe
　　of fire.
He heard his mother sing sweetly, his father's voice rose in
　　the air—
Now he was lonely and dying, with no kind form near him
　　to care !
　　　　A mist came over his vision,
　　　　　　A whisper stole soft in his ear ;
　　　　Above him, a fair form hovered,
　　　　　　And a voice whispered sweet and clear—
　　　　" My brother, your course is ended,
　　　　　　And your race here on earth is done ;
　　　　The fight has been fought and finished,
　　　　　　And the victory now is won !
　　　　When I was a child, you gave me,
　　　　　　When wandering lonely and sad,
　　　　Some bread to keep me from starving,
　　　　　　And kind smiles which made me feel glad.
　　　　Look up, and fear not, my brother !
　　　　　　Thy deeds are recorded above,
　　　　On tablets on high engraven
　　　　　　By One who does all things in love."
　　　　The earth from his vision faded,
　　　　　　A ray, like a light from the cross,
　　　　Fell over his face—then silence—
　　　　　　He'd suffer on earth no more loss.

A RED ROSE.

Lines on receiving one from a distance.

Away in the south, where the flowers bloom fair,
And the nightingale's song is heard in the air ;
When daylight retires with a solemn adieu,
And clouds above blush with a beautiful hue.

'Tis sweet when afar from the friends we love dear,
And sitting with thoughts that are sorrowful, drear,
To awake from our dreams and find at our side
A token of love, while our hearts fill with pride.

'Twas only a flower, a tiny red rose,
Which seemed to be sleeping, and blushed in repose
As it lay in a box which came from afar,
Yet brightened our eyes like a glorious star.

We read in the emblem a lesson of love
As pure, undefiled, as the sky up above—
A breath from the ocean of thought from a heart
Which welcomes a meeting and grieves to depart.

The rose now has faded, its petals are dead,
Its beauty has vanished, its freshness all fled ;
But yet a sweet perfume it sheds on the air,
Which tells of a treasure surpassingly rare.

The flowers must perish as seasons roll on,
And joys quickly wither, too soon are they gone ;
But a red faded flower we'll treasure and keep
Till we meet once again great gladness to reap.

THE SEWING MACHINE.

" MAN, Henry, just marry, an' tak' a bit wife,
To keep you aye cheery the hale o' your life ;
She'll keep you an' guide you, an' comfort you tae,
An' mak you feel happy throughout ilka day."

I kent a nice lassie, whose bonnie blue een
Played havoc within me, altho' 'twas unseen,—
But mony sair hearts lie hidden atweel
Beneath a calm surface, while anguish we feel.

I spiered at her plainly, if she'd become mine—
She looked at me fondly, and said, " I am thine,"—
I preed her bit mou', which was wonnerfu' sweet ;
Delicious it is tho' when lovers lips meet !

Fu' quick got we married, an' happy was I,
Contentment reigned round us, but soon bade good-bye ;
For yaumerin' weans cam' disturbin' my rest—
But Providence shapes ilka thing for the best.

The weans were aft greetin' frae mornin' till nicht,
Aye girnin' an' wheengin'—a sair waesome sicht ;
My wife at the flytin', her tongue micht clip clouts ;
The married man happy—I aye had my doots.

Cauld parritch to breakfast, wi' plenty sour dook ;
An' yet if I spak' out or ga'e her a look,
She opened her batteries, fired richt an' left—
I seemed for a while oft a' senses bereft.

At last, hoo it happened I hardly can tell,
But quicker than usual my head it got bell ;
I limped on ae fit too, but what do I care?
The marriage life's happy, an' I get my share !

The women tak' fancies to men aften whiles,
An' laugh braw an' hearty wi' face fu' o' smiles ;
But when they get married wreathes vanish awa',
Their temper tak's turns oft which naething can thaw.

My wife she cam' wheedlin' ae nicht to my side,
Dressed up like a duchess, an' in her nae pride !
An' said, while she glanced sly at me wi' her een,
" I think noo, dear Henry, I'll need a machine !"

Some men are like butter an' easy impress'd ;
The women are angels—but far frae their nest ;
An' Adam was foolish to tak' hame a mate—
It cost us (ye a' ken) a happy estate.

I got the machine, an' frae mornin' till nicht,
My house was like Bedlam, for naething was richt;
The taties were boilt saft like parritch or brose,
The meat like a cinder— to comfort the nose.

I suffered in silence for mony a day,
My health it was failin', my hair gettin' grey ;
A stoop i' my shouthers, an' unco bad hoast,
An' like what I was ance, just nocht but a ghost.

Ae nicht I determined to speak to the wife,
But oh ! I felt terribly feared o' my life ;
For women are generals—born to command—
An' mak' mony dacent chiels come to a stand.

F

I spak' out quite plainly, " Confound your machine !
I wish you would keep this bit house o' yours clean ;
An' no be aye sewin' an' ca'in awa',
When I'm earnin' siller to keep you fu' braw."

" Confound your machine !—ay ! you're very polite !
Of course, my dear husband, you always are right ;
But just let me tell you, *my* sewin' machine
I'll work at it ever as long's I ha'e een."

I sighed unco deeply, an' gazed in the fire,
An' houped that my wife o' her workin' would tire ;
But constantly, ever, ilk hour o' the day
My wife at her sewin' kept peggin' away.

The sewin' machine was a nichtmare to me,
For sleepin' or wakin' it aye I did see ;
An' heard it gang wheezin' an' buzzin' awa'—
I couldna stand't langer—what man could at a'?

I rose in the mornin' an' took the machine
Awa' to the back yaird, an' smashed it up clean ;
Then crept to my bed wi' a heart quakin' sair,
A voice whisp'rin' in me, " You'll need to take care."

I heard my wife risin', sae snored loud an' lang,
But sune it was changed to a different sang ;
A skelp on my haffits, wi' stars frae my een,
An' then a voice cryin', " Noo, whaur's my machine ? "

" Wha wants your machine ?" I cried out fu' o' pain,
When swiftly there came to my bedside amain,
A toaster an' poker, a dunt o' hard coal,
Which made me near senseless, scarce mair I could thole.

The bellows cam' fleein', an' struck on the wa',
An' then cam' a hammer as neat as a ba',
An' drove itsel' sairly against my puir head—
The married life happy ! I wish I was dead !

My wife cam' hersel' next, an' tugged at my hair,
An' cried out, "you villain," while thumpin' me sair ;
But women are gentle, so meek and so good,
A pity they live here on our earthly food.

" You've smashed my machine a' to splinters an' bits ;
You scoundrel, you blackguard, you'll drive me to fits ! "
Exhausted she halted, an' gasped sair for breath—
I dressed mysel' quickly in fear o' my death.

I bolted out suddenly up to the toun,
An' felt whizzin' past me a pair of auld shoon—
It's best to be married, an' ken a gude wife,
Wha'll keep you frae wearying a' thro' your life !

Noo tak' my advice a', ne'er marry before
You calculate earnestly what is in store ;
But if you want mony a lively bit scene,
When ance you are married—then buy a machine !

A HALF-BLOWN ROSE.

I.

A PAIR of wistful eyes,
　　That gaze on a childish face ;
A heart within which often cries,
　　As she sits in a well-known place.
And like to the evening's close,
When skies blush sweet in repose ;
　　　So a girl now sleeps
　　　While a mother keeps
A watch, while she strives to hide her woes.

II.

Softly the sun's rays gleam,
　　And quiver in streams of light,
While there strayeth a golden beam
　　Into the room with delight.
Kissing the ruby lips,
It steals o'er her face and finger tips ;
　　　And then it soon flies,
　　　Recedes fast and dies,
As the clouds its brilliant light eclipse.

III.

The bird in its cage sweet sings
　　A song from out its heart,
Yet, as it melody flings,
　　Each note's like a painful dart.

And the dog on the hearth lies low
And moans, as it stirs to and fro,
   And gazeth with eyes
   Where dumb anguish lies,
While the western zephyrs outside blow low.

IV.

'Tis the hush of eventide,
  A solemn silence broods
O'er the village, its valleys, and sleeps
  Away down in the shady woods.
As a spark leaps up, then dies,
So, unseen, the child's spirit flies
   To the realms of light,
   Where are spirits bright,
In mansions above the starry skies.

V.

The brightest flowers fade away,
  Treasures we fain would keep ;
We long for the light of day,
  And with pent-up tears we weep.
Down in the churchyard lone,
Where the night winds sob and moan,
   Is a little grave,
   Where grasses green wave,
And a rose now half unblown !

SUNSET.

THE sun is sinking in the west
And making clouds around to blush.
    As parting day
    Hies close away,
An evening hymn sweet sings the thrush ;
    While trees let fall
    Their shadows tall,
Like giant phantoms to the earth,
    And all is calm
    Which brings a balm
To hearts that tire of noisy mirth.

The wind breathes gently on the pool,
Caressing all its surface o'er ;
    While, like a fringe,
    A golden tinge
Dyes all the waters by the shore.
    And flowers close
    For sweet repose
Their weary eyelids for a while ;
    While up above
    The sky with love
Looks down on all with happy smile.

The heavens on high a deeper red,
Are arching o'er the vault of night,
    As sinks the sun,
    Its duty done,
While fades away the pure day light.
    O'er all the hills
    A vapour fills

Each lovely glen and valley near.
 While carols cease,
 And cometh peace,
Till nothing jars upon the ear.

The red light fades. The clouds rise up
No larger than a tiny hand,
 But quickly spread
 Fast overhead
In masses large, majestic grand ;
 And like a pall
 Soon covers all
With mantle of an inky hue,
 And night comes fast
 And swift at last,
As daylight bids to all adieu !

JESSIE.

I.

SMILING and coaxing
 The mother stands,
Watching her infant go crossing the floor,
While father is standing close to the door,
 And gleefully clapping loud his hands.
  Stepping out gently
  The child comes near,
And laughs to herself, with her bright clear eyes,
That have caught a reflection from azure skies—
 There's not in the wide world a baby so dear.

II.

Lovingly, warmly
Laid in her nest,
Jessie is slumbering, smiles in her sleep,
While around her cradle the angels keep
A watchful guard, as she lies at rest.
Her face is so calm,
I seem to see
The same Christ who spoke in the days of old,
And uttered aloud those words, precious as gold,—
"Oh ! suffer the children to come unto Me."

III.

Bright as the morning
Jessie awakes,
While she babbles and talks in unknown tongue,
As if at her birth here the fairies had sung,
And thus of their joys she too partakes.
What will she grow to
I ask full oft,
As I watch my child with her winning ways ;
And I list to the answering voice which says,
There's One who will guide her who dwelleth aloft.

IV.

So, just as Jessie
Cometh to me,
And pillows her head content on my breast,
And findeth with me a haven and rest,
And there for a time from woes is free.

In similar faith,
Through good and ill,
I will trust Him always to guide her ways,
Who calmeth the tempest and fear all allays,
By the simple uttering of " Peace, be still ! "

THE MAIDEN'S CONFESSION.

I.

I CANNOT tell thee all I feel,
For my brain seems in a whirl,
And my heart is loudly beating,—
I'm a foolish, foolish girl.
But his voice it sounded sweetly,
And his words I hear them still,
For he spoke to me so fondly—
My own handsome, dear, sweet Will !

II.

And he gazed at me so loving
With his eyes, which looked in mine,
As we stood alone together,
While the moon on high did shine.
But the time passed far too quickly—
Too quickly it sped for me ;
I think I could dwell for ever
With dear Will, and happy be.

III.

But men, I am told, are fickle,
  When a prettier face they see ;
But where are *any* more handsome,
  Or better looking than *me ?*
I'm sure I know of no other
  Than can e'er with me compare ;
For dear Will himself hath told me,
  He never saw one so fair.

IV.

Yet still I'm all in a flutter,
  For Will has been to papa ;
And I know what it is he wants,
  So I went and told mamma !
And now we're soon to be married,
  And I'm sure we'll happy be ;
For Will he'll make a nice husband,
  And I a good wife, you'll see !

THOSE BOYS.

I.

In her eyes was troublous dreaming,
  In her heart were hopes and fears,
And there came no light or gleaming—
  Not a glimpse of future years.

And she sat within the room,
Thicker, denser grew the gloom,
While she thought of vanished joys—
    'Twas a mother's whisper only,
    Sitting in the gloaming lonely—
Who will watch my orphan boys?

II.

In her lap her hands were lying,
    Fingers clasped together there;
Through the chinks the wind came sighing,
    Tempests brooding in the air.
In the sun's rays softly came,
Streamed like threads of crimson flame;
On the floor were childish toys,
    Many too of these were broken—
    Would there come to her no token,
Who would watch her infant boys?

III.

Memories came surging, thronging,
    In her eyes were welling tears;
While a wistful yearning, longing,
    Boomed and echoed in her ears.
Suddenly there came in sight
Something wrapped in mantle white—
Indistinctly did she see.
    Who is this that is attending,
    At her feet the figure's bending:
" Mamma, will God care for me?"

IV.

In her eyes a new light's beaming
   Bright and pure and shining clear ;
Surely she has but been dreaming,
   Wherefore all her doubt and fear ?
Soon she takes the child to pray,
Sorrows fly like mists away,
And her heart is filled with joys
     As she at the bedside kneeling
     Whispers thus with happy feeling :
" God will watch my orphan boys ! "

SONG—A WESTERN GEM.

Air—" O' a' the airts."

'TIS sweet to see in early morn
   The sun rise o'er the hills,
To hear the rippling waters lauch
   In a' the sparklin' rills ;
To hear the soughin' o' the win',
   The birds a' warblin' clear ;
But greater pleasures I aye ha'e
   When Mary, love, is near !

I like the glint o' Mary's een
   Which lichten up her face ;
They leave impressions on my heart
   Which time can ne'er deface.

In a' she does a glamour lies,
　In ilk thing is a spell ;
An' when she speaks her voice it soun's
　As clear's a marriage bell.

The lavcrock sings fu' joyous, sweet,
　When soarin' high in air,
As if the warl' was fu' o' love,
　Wi' ne'er a streak o' care.
An' Mary sings wi' syren's pow'r
　In ilka lilt I hear ;
She maks my heart gang pit-a-pat,—
　I whiles let fa' a tear.

The warl' is wide, an' gowd's a king
　Wha rules baith young an' auld ;
But gi'e me ae fond heart to lo'e,
　I'd suffer puirtith's cauld.
For Mary is as untold wealth,
　A treasure rich and rare ;
I trow there's nane I've ever seen,
　Wha would wi' her compare.

Oh ! sing ye wimplin' burns a sang,
　An' sing ilk bird an' bee,
An' waft the tokens o' my love
　To Mary, dear, frae me.
I see her face where'er I gang,
　Her bonnie lichtsome een,
They shine like diamonds in the sky,
　Set in an azure sheen.

Let ithers dream o' wealth an' fame,
　An' think o' gettin' gear,
An' grasp a bubble in their haun'
　To melt an' disappear.

I'll treasure deep doun i' my heart,
  The face I lo'e the best ;
O, Mary, dear, the brightest gem
  That e'er shone in the west !

RUMMLEGUMPTION.

My mither often spak' to me
  O' bygane days,
Concernin' Scotlan' an' her men,
  An' would them praise.
She tauld o' hoo they focht an' bled,
  Baith sire and son ;
An' proved themsel's a' leal an' true,
  An' freedom won.

She'd point to whaur the Pentlan' hills
  Stood firm an' sure ;
An' whaur on grassy Rullion Green,
  To keep aye pure
Religion from attendant vice,
  Oor men fell fast ;
An' noo in quietness Him we praise—
  Long may it last !

But noo-a-days oor younger men
  Lo'e pleasure mair
Than did our faithers' sires langsyne,
  An' dinna care

To gang to hear the Word o' Life
    Ilk Sabbath day,
But lounge at hame, or loll an' gant
    Their time away.

Nae rummlegumption some ha'e got,
    An' even leave
Their Bible frae ilk day to day,
    An' dinna grieve
That they ne'er turn its leaves or read
    What's writ therein ;
While dust oft gi'est a coatin' thick—
    The mair's their sin.

Oor forefaithers, thro' snaw an' show'r,
    In rain or sleet,
Would walk long weary miles to hear
    (Wi' hackit feet)
The Word o' God.   Their canopy
    The clouds an' sky,
Their seats the heather an' the grass,
    Yet—He was nigh.

But noo folk are ashamed to gang,
    Unless they're drest
In claes o' faultless shape, and mak'
    The very best.
A wee bit show'r keeps them awa',—
    Tho' some will gang,
When rain is pourin' quick an' fast,
    To hear a sang.

Ay, rummlegumption is a word
    Few comprehend,—
It just means plenty common sense—
    Oh ! would folk mend !

But like as apples so are men,
    For some are sour ;
An' ithers want a fusshen too,
    Men's hearts are dour.

The earth is fu' o' bonny scenes
    An' flow'rets fair ;
An' He wha rules abune ower a',
    Tak's aye gude care.
But we, for a' His benefits,
    Gi'e little praise;
An' trifle oft oor time awa',
    In useless ways.

An' rummlegumption I would wish
    Ilk ane to ha'e,
An' ken the guid o' present time,
    Which fleets away.
The birds sing for the joys they feel,
    An' sings the burn ;
But mony men ne'er gi'e a grunt—
    Oh'! would such turn,

An' learn in ilka thing they see,
    To trace His haun' ;
An' then, perchance, the truth they'll learn
    An' in it staun'.
Then Scotlan' wi' her noble sons
    Will ever prove
A bulwark for the ancient faith,
    Which nocht can move.

SAMUEL SMILES JERDAN.

Died 26th February 1878.

THE spring was coming nearer,
 With garlands bright and gay ;
The winter's snow had vanish'd,
 With cold bleak winds away.
Fair flow'rs were peeping upwards
 From out the dark brown earth ;
While birds around were singing—
 All Nature full of mirth !

But one who oft sang clearly
 With heart attuned to praise,
And brightened many homesteads
 With joyous cheerful lays,
Was fading, fleeting, dying,
 In manhood's early prime,
Though joys were coming onwards
 To gladden this dark clime.

The harp is broken—silent,
 The singer's voice no more
Will cheer in accents joyous,
 As oft in days of yore.
Farewell ! but still thou leavest
 A noble name behind,
Of one aye true, leal-hearted,
 Whose ways were ever kind.

G

THE CLASP OF A HAND.

'TWAS only the clasp of a woman's hand,
    Tender and true,
With a look from eyes, with an azure light,
    Which thrilled me through,
And then we parted. But still I can see
    A sweet fond face,
And a little form in a dress of black.
    I yet can trace
The beseeching look, the tender adieu
    And kind farewell.
And when time has pass'd, and over my grave
    The sweet blue bell
With other flowers wave, then—but not till then —
    Will love be dead ;
Till the blood in my veins doth cease its flow,
    And life has fled,
Will I e'er forget that beautiful face,
    Or tender hand.
And then when I die may I meet her there,
    In yonder land.

GENEROSITY.

MISS TOMPKINS had a magpie once
    She loved with all her heart,
For no young man had ever asked
    To share that tender part !

Miss Tompkins was not very old,
   Her charms were yet quite green—
But beauty (like a flower) oft blooms,
   And flourishes *unseen!*

So all alone she wandered oft
   Within her garden drest ;
While magpie on her shoulder perched,
   Her dear and honoured guest.

One day the magpie on the ground
   Picked up a treasured prize,
Which in its bill it deftly hid,
   Unseen by mortal eyes.

Then gently up from earth it flew,
   And on her shoulder came ;
It seemed so full of love and joy
   It could not speak her name !

Miss Tompkins stroked it with her hand,
   And called it "just a dear ;"
Then held it closely to her lips,
   For no young man was near !

Then suddenly the magpie put
   Its bill between her lips;
But, like a foolish bird, it proved
   Its last and best eclipse !

For oh ! it dropped—how can I tell?
   But truth I will not hide—
A caterpillar, large and fat,
   Then hopped on by her side !

But from that day no bird is seen
  Miss Tompkins near at hand ;
Her gen'rous friend, the magpie's dead,
  Sent to another land !

"Ἄλλοι κάμον.

"Ἄλλοι κάμον, ἄλλοι ὤναντο —
This is a truth which all must know here.
Thousands ever are toiling, struggling,
Jogging along on this earthly sphere.
    Work, work,
    Work, work,
Tho' their bread be won with many a tear.

Ἄλλοι κάμον, ἄλλοι ὤναντο—
Some of us toil that others may reap ;
Hearts are breaking, children are starving,
While others around with grief sore weep,
    Weep, weep,
    Weep, weep,
Till slumber comes with its balmy sleep.

"Ἄλλοι κάμον, ἄλλοι ὤναντο—
Here for a space, and then we go—where ?
Some of us work, strive to be happy—
Toil till our hearts get broken or sere—
    Toil, toil,
    Toil, toil,
Toil aye, and struggle 'mid hope and fear.

"Ἄλλοι κάμον, ἄλλοι ὤναντο—
Riches are lent to fly soon away.
Many *must* work, and some, too, *must* weep,
Till the dawn is seen which seems to say—
"Ἄλλοι κάμον,
"Ἄλλοι ὤναντο,
What is life but a brief summer's day?

SONG—SWEET IS THE MORNIN'.

Air—" The Flowers o' the Forest."

I.

SWEET is the mornin' when Nature is adornin'
The earth wi' her garlands an' treasures so fair ;
When birds begin singing,
An' echoes are ringing,
Like syrens carolling some anthem full rare.
The winds are sighing, for pleasures are flying,
Too soon cometh darkness an' long hours o' care.
But Jessie will cheer me,
To all things endear me—
Even Winter, so grumlie, will frighten us ne'er.

II.

Flowers gay are blooming, in garb unassuming,
An' wafting a perfume both pleasant an' rare.
An' Jessie's aye smilin',
Her charms are beguilin',
While in a' her features there's no trace of care.

'Tis sweet in the gloamin', when we twa are roamin',
Our hearts are aye lichtsome an' feel nae a sair.
    We lo'e ane anither,
    So I will ne'er swither,
Sin' she's promised to me noo hersel' bright an' fair.

WHAT'S WRANG NOO?

WHAT'S wrang noo, my puir wee lassie,
    That you're greetin' there sae sair ;
Like to burst your wee heart sabbin'—
    Surely you can ha'e nae care ?
Such a waesome face, my lassie,
    Come an' tell me a' what's wrang ;
Look up, see the little birdie's
    Singing you a cheery sang.

II.

Dicht your een, then, but you're bonnie,
    You an' I will yet agree;
Tho' you're shy, gey blate an' bashfu',
    Keekin' ower your haun's at me.
Did you want your mither, lassie?
    Mither, see an' come quick hame,
For a little lass is waitin',
    Tired o' bein' a' her lane.

III.

See the cat ! Look hoo it's runnin',
　As its tail it tries to bite ;
Roun' an' roun' about its loupin',
　Surely pussy's gane clean gyte.
Noo it's got a ba' o' worset—
　Some great prize it thinks, nae doubt ;
An' it's got it a' entangled,
　Ravelled past the touzlin' oot.

IV.

Oh ! look yonder, such a wonder,
　There's anither little wean
In yon glass, wi' cheeks as rosy
　An' a face just like your ain.
Wha can't be, yon bonnie bairnie—
　Dae you think it is yoursel'?
Sae you've guessed it—weel that's clever,
　It's no every wean could tell.

V.

Ah ! there's mither—rin an' meet her ;
　Losh me ! there you've tummelled doun ;
Shoo, bad pussy--puir wee lassie,
　Fa'en an' hurt her little croun.
But she cares na, for her mither
　Lifts her quickly aff the floor ;
An' wi' kisses soothes her sorrows—
　Sune she's free frae childish care.

WHY THE SEA MOANS.

THE sea keeps surging throughout the day,
And on thro' the hours till twilight grey,
And laps the shore with its waters white,
Feathery flakelets pale with affright ;
While sobbing aloud in monotone,
For the sea is cold, and all alone.

II.

A weary cry from the forest dim
Came surging along like some sad hymn,
And rippling on thro' the autumn air,
With a deathless wail of great despair ;
It joins its cry where the wild waves rolled
By the bleak sea-shore so damp and cold.

III.

And a legend tells that long ago,
When spirits unseen went to and fro,
And reigned in their kingdoms ruling well,
And whose voices rose in tuneful swell,
That went o'er the earth in rippling song,
Like echoes sweet from a starry throng.

IV.

The Sea-king longed for the forest Queen,
(He saw her afar in pearly sheen),

And he sang aloud and praised her eyes
Like rubies from out the azure skies ;
And spoke of a love never to die—
And softly there came a sweet reply :—

V.

" Oh ! King, thou'rt fairer, more dear to me,
Than the coral caves, joy of the sea !
Come to me now, for I roam at night
In darkness often, and long for light—
For thou art to me my guiding star,
And I hear thy loved voice from afar."

VI.

Then gladly the spirit of the sea
Over the waters sped in his glee ;
He bathed his face in the bright sea foam,
And thought of the bride he'd soon bring home ;
And then in his joy came to the shore,
Where the waves rolled on with muffled roar.

VII.

The Queen of the forest tried to reach
The spirit King who roamed by the beach ;
But they could not meet there side by side,
For in their kingdoms each had to bide.
So they parted there with fond good-bye,
While over the sea there sped a sigh !

VIII.

So ever since then the sea sad moans,
And echoes aloud its sobs and groans ;
While the forest Queen doth ever sigh,
When thro' her dominions passing by !—
Thus the ocean King and forest Queen,
Grieve in despair for what might have been.

COMMERCIAL PRINTING COMPANY, EDINBURGH.